For Satoshi and Yoko

SIMON & SCHUSTER BOOKS FOR YOUNG READERS
Simon & Schuster Building, Rockefeller Center, 1230 Avenue of the Americas,
New York, New York 10020. Copyright © 1991 by David McKee.
Originally published in Great Britain by Andersen Press, Ltd. First U.S. edition 1993.
All rights reserved including the right of reproduction in whole or in part in any form.
SIMON & SCHUSTER BOOKS FOR YOUNG READERS is a trademark of Simon & Schuster.
Manufactured in Italy
10 9 8 7 6 5 4 3 2 1
Library of Congress Cataloging-in-Publication Data
McKee, David. Zebra's hiccups/by David McKee.   p.   cm.
Summary: When Zebra gets the hiccups, all his animal
friends have cures to suggest.
[1. Hiccups—Fiction.   2. Zebras—Fiction.   3. Animals—Fiction.]
I. Title.   PZ7.M19448Ze   1993   [E]—dc20   92-14453   CIP
ISBN: 0-671-79440-X

David McKee
ZEBRA'S HICCUPS

SIMON & SCHUSTER BOOKS FOR YOUNG READERS
Published by Simon & Schuster
New York • London • Toronto • Sydney • Tokyo • Singapore

The animals loved to play.
"Come and play, Zebra," they called. "We're having fun."
"No, thank you, I am busy," Zebra answered. He was a *very* serious and dignified zebra.

One day Zebra got the hiccups.
"Oh my, how inconvenient H I C ," he said to himself. "I will simply H I C ignore them and go out for a walk. Perhaps they will disappear."

"Hi there, Zebra," said Tiger.
"Good H_1C , good morning H_1C ," said Zebra.
"Hiccups!" said Tiger. "I know just the cure. Hold your breath, close your eyes, and say the alphabet backwards."
"That is too silly to H_1C work," said Zebra.

"Yoo-hoo, Zebra," called Miss Pig. "Come skating with me."
"Good morning, Miss H₁C ," said Zebra.
"Hiccups?" asked Miss Pig. "I have just the thing. Put your head between your knees and drink a glass of water upside down."
"No H₁C you," said Zebra. "That is far too un H₁C dignified for me."

"Zebra's got the hiccups," said Little Elephant. "When I get the hiccups
I hop on one leg and say *too d'loo d'loo d'loo* as long as I can."
"Me, too," said Big Elephant.
"That would never H I C do," said Zebra.

Next, Zebra met Crocodile.

"Shoot baskets with me," said Crocodile.

"No, thank you Croco $H_I C$," said Zebra.

"Uh-oh, who has the hiccups?" said Crocodile. "Here's a sure-fire hicketty cure. Stand on your head, hold this ball between your legs and sing! Works every time."

"Not $H^I C$ for this zebra," said Zebra.

Then something strange began to happen. The hiccupping began to move Zebra's stripes. The more he hiccupped, the more his stripes bumped together. Zebra never noticed.

It was Mrs. Duck who told him.
"Is that you, Zebra?" she asked. "You do look strange."
"You mean H*I*C *sound* strange," said Zebra. "It's the hiccups."
"I mean *look* strange. Look at yourself," said Mrs. Duck.

"OH, NO!" groaned Zebra. "Look what has happened. My wonderful stripes. I look H_1C diculous."

"I should have tried those cures," thought Zebra. "What was it Tiger suggested? I can't remember." He hurried back to find Tiger.

At Tiger's house, Zebra took a deep breath, closed his eyes, and said, "Z Y X V, no W H¡C . Oh, no, H¡C ! I mean ZYXWVUT H¡C RS, no, SR H¡C ."

Tiger started to giggle. Zebra opened his eyes.
"This isn't working," he said. "I'm off H_1C to see Miss Pig. It's not H^1C
funny, you know."
"Well, I think it's very funny," said Tiger, "Wait for me."

Miss Pig gave Zebra a glass of water. "Put your head between your knees and drink this upside down," she said.
Zebra sat and drank, but it only made him cough and sputter and choke and...
HIc cup!

"Absolu HIC ly hopeless, and very HIC messy," said Zebra with a little smile. "Maybe Elephant's cure will work."

"I'll help you, Zebra," said Little Elephant. "Hop on one leg and *too d'loo* as long as you can."
Zebra went "*Too d'loo d'* HIC *d'loo d'loo* HIC *loo* H$_I$C " until the others were laughing aloud.

Zebra grinned. "Totally HIC useless. Come on, let's see if HIC odile's cure can stop these hicketty HIC cups."

"First do a headstand," said Crocodile. "Put the ball between your legs. Now, *sing!*"
Zebra just started laughing.

"My cure doesn't work if you laugh," said Crocodile.
"I can't help H_IC it," said Zebra, falling over in a fit of giggles.

Mrs. Duck came along to see what all the noise was about.
"He can't hiccup forever," she said. "I know just what we should do."
She whispered her plan to the others.

Zebra was still laughing. Suddenly, he was drenched with six buckets of cold water.
"Now that's *not* funny," he said.
But there was not one HIC.

"It worked! He's cured," cried Mrs. Duck excitedly.
"Hooray!" shouted all the animals.
"Thank goodness my hiccups are gone," said Zebra. "But I do feel strange without my stripes."

Zebra shivered and sneezed a huge sneeze. That did the trick—it shook all his stripes back into place.
"Two cures in one," said Zebra. "Thank you A C H O   O all."

"You're catching a cold," said Tiger. "I know a great cure."
"So do I, so do I," the others all shouted.
"And so do I," Zebra laughed. He waved goodbye to his new friends and hurried home to a steaming bath, some hot cocoa, and a nice warm bed.